To Steve, who has always helped me produce great things, including Nicole, Jenn, Kristyn, and now my first published book.

– AI

www.mascotbooks.com

Let's Vote! A Fruitful Election Tale

©2016 Anita Iaco. All Rights Reserved. No part of this publication may be reproduced, stored in a retrieval system or transmitted in any form by any means electronic, mechanical, or photocopying, recording or otherwise without the permission of the author.

For more information, please contact:
Mascot Books
560 Herndon Parkway #120
Herndon, VA 20170
info@mascotbooks.com

Library of Congress Control Number: 2016907875

CPSIA Code: PRT0616A
ISBN-13: 978-1-63177-732-5

Printed in the United States

Let's VOTE!

A Fruitful Election Tale

by Anita Iaco • Illustrated by Chiara Civati

As the students entered Miss Jenn's classroom one early November day, they were surprised at what they saw on the table.

Instead of the colorful picture books that usually greeted them, there were some apples, bananas, and oranges.

When everyone arrived, Miss Jenn announced, "It's Election Day. Grown-ups around the United States are going to vote for the people they want to help run the country.

"Today, you will get to vote too—for your favorite fruit. You'll take the ballot card with the picture of your favorite fruit on it and vote by putting the card in the election box. At the end of the day, the fruit with the most votes will be given the title of class fruit!

Danielle raised her hand and quickly announced,
"My favorite fruit is the banana!"

"Okay, Danielle. Since fruit can't talk, you can speak
for the banana. You will be its campaign spokesperson,"
said Miss Jenn. "You'll have to make a speech to tell
everyone why the banana is so great and ask them to
vote for that fruit."

Marcos became the orange's campaign spokesperson. And since Kristyn knew the apple had a certain appeal, she agreed to speak for that fruit. Miss Jenn gave all three students an apple, orange, and banana. She also gave them supplies to make posters and told them they would make their speeches after lunch.

Danielle was the first one to speak to the class. "Bananas are easy to peel, easy to eat, and taste very sweet," she said with a big grin. Then she broke up her banana and gave it out to her fellow classmates.

Agreeing with Danielle, some students asked for more bananas. But she had no more to give out. "If the banana gets the most votes, I promise I'll give everyone a banana tomorrow. So you should vote for the delicious banana!" Danielle said.

"Wait a minute," said Miss Jenn. "What if the store is closed when you get there? Or what if it's out of bananas? You may not be able to keep that promise, and your classmates might be disappointed. They'll have a hard time believing you again."

Danielle thought for a moment and realized her teacher was right. "I will *try* to bring in bananas tomorrow," she said.

Then it was Marcos' turn.

"This banana has brown blotches and streaks and its stem is broken," Marcos said holding up the fruit. "And look, the apple has a few soft spots that are darker than the rest of the skin. You don't want to pick a fruit that is ugly and broken. It can be rotten inside and might make you sick! So you should vote for the beautiful orange," he proclaimed.

"That is not true," Albert pointed out. "Yesterday, I ate an apple that had a brown spot. It still tasted good, and I didn't throw up."

Miss Jenn warned, "We shouldn't make choices based on what something looks like on the outside. And we shouldn't say the wrong things just because we want to win. Just be honest, Marcos."

Marcos said, "Like how oranges are full of vitamin C and taste like candy?" The students smiled and clapped when they heard the word "candy."

"Wow. I didn't need to say bad things about those other fruits," Marcos admitted. "I just had to tell the truth about oranges."

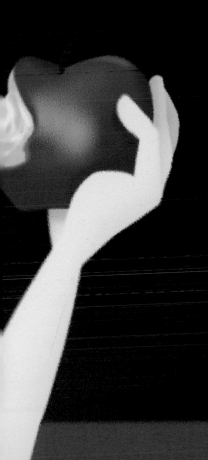

Kristyn got up next.

"Apples don't need to be peeled to be eaten," she said, taking a big bite out of her apple. "They are good for your body too because they have fiber. *And* if you vote for the other fruit, I will *not* be your friend!" she said, her voice turning grumpy. "So, you better vote for the crunchy apple!"

"You sound like a bully!" shouted Nicole. "What if no one votes for the apple? Then you won't have anyone to play with."

Kristyn wanted the apple to win but didn't want to lose her friends. "I'm sorry. *Please* vote for the apple."

It was time for the students to cast their votes. Miss Jenn counted the ballots and congratulated the campaign spokespeople for realizing how important it is to make promises you can keep, to tell the truth, and to be nice.

Then she announced the winner. It was...

The banana!

Kristyn and Marcos were disappointed their fruit didn't win, but they shook Danielle's hand and said they would gladly eat bananas.

When her dad picked Danielle up after school, she told him all about the election and how much fun she had speaking for the banana. He offered to take Danielle to the store to buy a treat for helping her favorite fruit win. What did she ask for?

"Well, since I can't buy an election," Danielle said laughing, "how about a bunch of bananas to share with all of my friends?"

Which fruit would you choose?

Cast your vote at
www.anitaiaco.com/vote

About the Author

Anita Iaco, aka "Mom" and "Miss Anita," owns a preschool in North Haledon, New Jersey, with her daughter Jenn and their family. Their little students gift her with funny, sentimental, and inspirational story ideas almost daily. She hopes this is the first of many picture books she can create and share with parents and children near and far.

Anita met her husband Steve at Iona College where she graduated with a degree in Communications Arts. Anita and Steve will forever be grateful to the college for bringing them together and helping them launch an amazing journey.

They live in Wayne, New Jersey.

Find out more about Anita and her preschool at www.anitaiaco.com and www.jennsjunction.com